THE ADVENTURES OF LILY MOO

Deanna McKinney

AuthorHouse™
1663 Liberty Drive
Bloomington, IN 47403
www.authorhouse.com
Phone: 1 (800) 839-8640

Because of the dynamic nature of the Internet, any web addresses or links contained in this book may have changed since publication and may no longer be valid. The views expressed in this work are solely those of the author and do not necessarily reflect the views of the publisher, and the publisher hereby disclaims any responsibility for them.

Any people depicted in stock imagery provided by Getty Images are models,
and such images are being used for illustrative purposes only.
Certain stock imagery © Getty Images.

This book is printed on acid-free paper.

ISBN: 978-1-7283-2671-9 (sc)
ISBN: 978-1-7283-2672-6 (e)

Print information available on the last page.

Published by AuthorHouse 09/09/2019

authorHOUSE®

THE ADVENTURES OF LILY MOO

THE ADVENTURES OF LILY MOO

Lily Moo was a little black and white mouse who lived in a cage with two other mice named Flakey and Lady DeWinter. The three mice belonged to twin girls named Leanne and Lotte. Flakey was a slim little mouse, always running on the exercise wheel. Lady DeWinter burrowed through the wood chips in the cage all the time. But Lily Moo was a rather lazy little mouse, and was content to sleep and eat. She rarely used the exercise wheel. When Leanne or Lotte would clean the mouse cage, they had to be quick to catch Flakey or Lady DeWinter. But Lily Moo was easy to catch! Lady DeWinter liked to climb, and Flakey was very quick, so the girls had to watch closely when the cage door was open. But Lily Moo never even tried to escape.

One day Leanne was getting ready to clean the cage. It was a pretty day, and Leanne was trying to hurry. She wanted to be outside! "Hmmm, let's see," she said, "I'll see if I can catch Lady DeWinter or Flakey first. They're harder to catch than Lily Moo. Lily's a lazy little mouse!" Lily Moo looked up from the piece of apple she was nibbling and thought, "I am tired of being called lazy!!" It made her angry, but she wasn't sure what to do about it. Leanne had taken Lady DeWinter out of the cage and put her in the pet carrier. It took a little time, but she had finally caught Flakey when the phone rang.

Leanne put Flakey in the carrier and ran to the phone. In her hurry, she didn't remember right away that she had left the cage door open. And when she did remember, she thought, "Oh, Lily Moo will be all right for a few minutes."

While Leanne was talking, Lily Moo looked at the open door. "This is my chance to show them!" she thought. And for the first time, Lily was curious about what was outside the cage! She walked over . . . and looked out the door and around the room. Everything was quiet, except for the sound of Leanne's voice on the phone. Lily Moo crept through the doorway.

The mouse cage was sitting on the floor of the bedroom, so Lily Moo stepped right onto the carpet. It was a new feeling on her feet, so she walked slowly and carefully. After a few steps, Lily decided she liked the feel. She took one step, and another, and another and then another! Just like that, she was standing in the bedroom doorway. A long hall stretched in front of her.

Lily Moo looked to the right. There were more rooms. She looked to the left. There were rooms that way, too. Lily scampered off to the right.

The first door she came to led to another bedroom. It belonged to Staci, Leanne and Lotte's big sister. There were so many things to see in this room! She wandered all over the room, around shoes, books, and papers. The papers made a crackly noise that Lily Moo liked when she walked over them. She began to run back and forth across them, again and again, having great fun! Soon Staci's neat pile of papers were scattered everywhere!

After she left Staci's room, Lily came to another bedroom. This room was where Kevin, the girls' brother, slept. Kevin's room had socks, jeans, and shoes thrown everywhere! In one corner laid his baseball and glove. Lily scampered all round the room, quietly looking at everything. She thought the color of the jeans was pretty, and nibbled them to see if they tasted good. They didn't. The baseball glove looked interesting. She nibbled it, but it tasted terrible. Lily sniffed at Kevin's sneaker. It smelled so bad she didn't even nibble at it! Finally she gave up and left Kevin's room.

By now Lily Moo was tired and wanted a place to sleep. The long hallway seemed like such a great adventure earlier, but now it just looked long. Lily thought about her cage, and remembered the smell of the wood chips. She wished that she could burrow down in them right now and take a nap!

Lily Moo scampered up and down the hall, twitching her whiskers. Then off she went! She scampered down the hall, away from Kevin's room. Past Staci's room. At last Lily came to Leanne and Lotte's room. Leanne was still on the phone, and the room was just like it had been when Lily Moo left! It seemed to her that she'd been gone a long time, even though she really hadn't.

Flakey and Lady DeWinter watched form the pet carrier as Lily made her way over to the cage and went inside. By the time Leanne came back, Lily Moo was fast asleep in the wood chips. "Just as I thought, Lily Moo," Leanne sighed in relief. "You didn't go anywhere. You're too lazy." Lily Moo opened one little black eye, looked at Leanne, and sighed too.

LILY MOO AND THE NAP QUEST

Lily Moo was a cranky mouse. It was a beautiful fall afternoon. The sun shone in the window, making it perfect for napping. So why was Lily Moo grumbling instead of snuggled down into the wood chips, fast asleep? "Pee-YEW!!! These wood chips stink. Leanne hasn't changed them in just forever!" Lilly huffed. Leanne and her sister Lotte were the owners of Lily Moo and her friends Flakey and Lady DeWinter. Usually they took good care of the mice, but lately both girls had been so busy! Flakey didn't miss a step on the exercise wheel as she said, "I don't smell anything, Lily." "Of course you don't," Lily Moo muttered to herself, "you never slow down long enough for the smell to catch up with you!" Lady DeWinter looked up from rummaging around the cage floor. A wood chip was sticking to her nose. Lady De sneezed and said, "I seeb to hab godden a code. I cad sbell it eider." Lily shrugged sympathetically and twitched her nose. How could a mouse get any sleep like this? In a rare burst of energy, Lily Moo kicked the cage door. Much to her surprise, it came open! Lily's eyes grew big for a moment. She looked at Lady DeWinter, sniffling and snuffling in a corner. She looked at Flakey, who hadn't even slowed down. "I'm out of here," Lily tossed over her shoulder as she climbed out of the cage. It took a bit of effort, since mice are not supposed to be able to get out, but get out she did. "Hmmmmm," Lily Moo said, "now where is a good napping place?" Spying Leanne's bed, she thought aloud, "Leanne sleeps there a lot . . . it must be comfortable." So Lily grabbed ahold of the big, fluffy comforter and up she went. "Man," she puffed upon reaching the top, "I am ready for a nap now!" But when she curled up on the comforter, the sum beaming in the window was warm. TOO warm. So down the comforter Lily Moo went, in search of the perfect napping place. She didn't find it in the hallway – no cozy places there! The bathroom was too wet and steamy – Leanne and Lotte's big sister Staci had just taken a shower. Lily peeked in Staci's room, thinking that one of Staci's many pillows sounded good. But Staci was blowdrying her hair – too NOISY!! In fact, every room Lily Moo looked in was either too noisy, too busy, or too uncomfortable! And in all her walking, Lily Moo was getting more and more tired. And hungry! "Well . . . maybe I'll just stop by the cage and have a bite to eat before I look any more," Lily decided. But getting back IN the cage proved to be even harder than getting OUT! Flakey noticed Lily Moo's efforts. "I'll help you, Lily!" she offered, and scurried over to where the cage door still stood open (since mice can't close them.) "Give me your paw," Flakey told Lily, "and I'll pull you in!" One . . . two . . . three! Flakey gave a hard tug. Nothing happened. Finally Lady DeWinter came sniffling and snuffling over to help. One . . . two . . . three! They both pulled. All three mice went flying backwards, landing on top of each other in a pile of wood chips. Everything was quiet for a few seconds. Lady De sneezed twice, blew the wood chips off her face, and wandered over to the water bottle for a drink. Flakey brushed herself off and looked at Lily Moo. "Are you okay, Lily?" "Yes . . . I'm all right. Th – thanks, Flakey," Lily Moo stammered. With a satisfied nod, Flakey trotted off to the exercise wheel. "I'll just rest for a second," Lily thought, "then get some food." But in a second . . . Lily Moo was fast asleep. And she was still asleep when Leanne came home later and found Flakey and Lady DeWinter poking curious noses out the open cage door. "Oh no you don't," she scolded as she fastened the door securely. "How did that get open," she wondered aloud. Leanne glanced at the sleeping Lily Moo and shook her head. "Figures that Lazy Lily Moo wouldn't even try to escape." Flakey and Lady De looked at each other and shrugged. Lily Moo gave a tiny, tired sigh, and with an offended "hmph," settled in to sleep some more.

CLEAN THE CAGE!

It was a beautiful spring morning. The bedroom windows were open, and birds could be heard singing happily. But in Leanne and Lotte's room it was not pleasant! "I cleaned the cage last time!" Leanne said. "This time it's YOUR turn!" "Oh, sure you cleaned it last time," Lotte replied, "but how many times did I clean it before then?" In the cage – the subject of this argument – were Lily Moo, Flakey, and Lady DeWinter. The three mice watched unnoticed as the argument became angrier and louder. Finally Lotte shouted, "I am NOT cleaning the cage!" and stomped out of the room. "Well, neither am I!" Leanne yelled after her. When Leanne left, slamming the door behing her, the three mice looked at each other. "What are we going to do?" Lily looked at the other two, who shrugged their shoulders and looked worried. "They didn't mean it," Flakey said, but she didn't sound very confident. "I – I'm sure you're right. The girls will take care of us," Lady De declared. "You'll see!" But the cage did not get cleaned that day. Or the next day. Or the next. Or the day after that. Leanne and Lotte were friendly again, and they made sure the mice had food and water. But neither of them would clean the cage. It got smellier and nastier as the days went by.

Sometimes Leanne or Lotte would comment on how the cage smelled, or that the bedroom was starting to stink. But the battle of who would clean the cage dragged on.

Lily, Lady De, and Flakey were very unhappy mice. Lily slept all the time. She began to look more like a black and gray mouse instead of the black and white mouse that she was. Lady De spent a lot of her time looking sadly towards the bedroom window, and her fur lost its healthy shine. Even energetic Flakey stopped running on her wheel. Her white fur was now very dingy from the dirty cage. None of them had much of an appetite any more, so the food just sat and added to the smell.

Finally one day Lily Moo heard the girls' mom in the hallway. Leanne and Lotte were trying to persuade her to take them to the mall later that day. "We'll see," Mom said. "After lunch, I want to see if your room is clean."

That gave Lily Moo and idea! She nudged Lady De awake. "I've **got** it!" she cried. "What . . ." Lady De mumbled. Lily nosed at Flakey, who was leaned up against Lady De, asleep. "We're going to get our cage cleaned," she declared. "How?" Flakey asked. "I have an idea," Lily Moo answered. She ran to the bars of the cage, turned and began to kick the wood chips. They flew up, out through the bars, and fell to the carpet. Flakey and Lady DeWinter got the idea and joined her. Wood chips flew **everywhere!** When the area by the bars was clean, Lily nosed more wood chips over while the other mice kicked them out. Soon they heard the girls and their mother coming. Mom stopped and looked at the pile of nasty, smelly, dirty wood chips on the floor. She looked at the three mice, who were looking up at her. After a minute, she looked at the girls. "When was the last time that cage was cleaned?" she asked in an angry voice. "It's her--" "Well,

I--" Mom held her hand up. "You girls have 10 minutes to sit down and decide how you are going to take care of your mice. I will be back to hear about it, and if I don't like your solution, the mice will go live somewhere else. Understood?" They nodded. Mom went on in a softer voice. "The mice are getting sick because they've not been taken care of. This" – she pointed to the pile of wood chips – "was their way of telling you." Then she left. Leanne reached into the cage for Flakey. A tear rolled down her cheek as she realized how neglected the mice were. Lotte played with Lady De for a minute, her eyes sad. Then she got Lily Moo. "We're sorry," she whispered to the mice. Mom came back to find both girls cleaning up the mess. She did take them to the mall after that, leaving three relieved mice in a clean cage. And though there were still disagreements sometimes about who would clean the cage, it always got done.

SOMETHING NEW, LILY MOO!

Lily Moo was feeling like a restless mouse. She had gotten good at sneaking out of the cage she shared with Flakey and Lady DeWinter to explore the house. But today their girls Leanne and Lotte were in no hurry to leave the room! Lily could see by the excited way the sisters talked that something big had happened. That made her even more anxious to get out and see what it was!

At last the girls left to eat breakfast. Lily listened as the family ate and then heard them leave, one by one. Lily Moo's whiskers twitched impatiently. When it was quiet, she trotted to the cage door and jiggled it. Lady DeWinter watched with mild interest as the latch clicked and the door came open.

Lily climbed out of the cage and looked around. "Let's look around a little bit," she said to herself. The hallway was quiet – nothing different there. Kevin's room was messy but that was nothing new, either. But Staci's room . . . it had something in front of the door. It looked kind of like a little gate. Lily Moo easily squeezed through the gate and looked around. Nothing else really looked different. "Hmph," Lily muttered. "I don't see anything that needs to be kept in here by a gate!" Just then she felt something touch her back. Something that was sort of cool and moist. Lily whirled around to find herself face to face with a little gray kitten who was sniffing at her with a mixture of curiosity and interest. Lily and the kitten stared at each other for few seconds. Everything was quiet, and it was as if time stopped. Then everything began to happen at once! Lily Moo screamed "YIPES!" and ran for the door. The kitten, frightened by Lily's scream, puffed up and hissed before running to hide under Staci's bed. Once she got out of the bedroom, Lily leaned against the wall shivering. As she calmed down, Lily's natural curiosity returned. She slowly turned and stretched to peek around the doorway into the bedroom. To her surprise, the kitten was peeking out! Lily froze, not sure what to do. Then the kitten said, "You're not going to scream again, are you? "N-no," Lily said. "You're not going to eat me, are you?" The kitten wrinkled her nose. "Yuk. No offense," she said quickly. "I don't like the taste of mouse." "Whew!" Lily sighed. "I think it's time for me to go catch a nap." "Come see me again anytime," the kitten said. "My name is Smoky." "Okay, I will, Smoky," Lily answered as she started back to her cage. She stopped, paused for a moment, then turned to ask, "What do you like the taste of?" Smoky smiled. "Chili. Oh, and pumpkin pie!" Lily nodded and waved goodbye. As she climbed into the cage, Flakey asked, "Are you okay? We heard you scream! What happened?" Lily sighed, "You wouldn't believe me if I told you."

PRETTY!

It was a rainy day. It was the kind of morning that causes a lot of people to oversleep. And that is exactly what happened to Leanne, Lotte, and their entire family. Everybody rushed around in a frenzy! Lotte was brushing her teeth while Leanne was trying to quickly put her hair in a ponytail. Staci was trying to reach her shoe from under the bed where Smoky had hidden it. Kevin was holding a shirt, sniffing it and looking it over, trying to decide, was it clean enough to wear, or would Mom make him change? The noise dwindled as one by one, the family got ready and went their separate ways to begin the day. Lady DeWinter slept right through the chaos, but Lily Moo watched it all, her bright eyes shining with interest. Staci stopped to talk to Leanne on her way out. "Here are the earrings you wanted to borrow, but if you want to ride with me, I'm leaving now." Leanne took the earrings and stuffed them in her pocket as she grabbed her backpack. "Thanks, I'll put them on in the car." The girls began chattering about the CD Staci wanted to buy after school, and only Lily noticed the earring that fell out of Leanne's pocket as they left. Lily nudged Flaky. "Did you see that? Leanne dropped something!" Flaky looked over to where Lily Moo pointed. "Can you eat it?" she asked. Lily rolled her eyes and laughed as she expertly jiggled the door to the cage until it opened. Creeping across the floor, she carefully looked over this thing the girls had called an earring. It was kind of dangly with bright sparkly stones in it. Lily Moo picked it up in her mouth and carried it back to the cage. Flaky sniffed it and, quickly losing interest, climbed into the running wheel. Lady De also looked it over and then scampered off in search of a snack. Lily shook her head. "It's pretty," she told them. She decided it would be neat to keep and look at once in awhile, so she tucked it safely away in the wood chips. Then, in a rare burst of energy, she chased Flaky on the wheel before taking a nap. She awoke to the sound of loud, angry voices. Staci was screaming at Leanne, and Leanne was yelling right back. "I can't believe you lost my earring! I will never let you borrow anything ever again!" "Staci, I told you I'd buy you a new pair! What else do you want from me?" "I want my earrings back!" Lady De burrowed down deeper into the wood chips, and Flaky ran harder on the wheel as Staci screamed on and on at Leanne. Finally, she left, slamming the door as Leanne cried on her bed. Lily Moo felt bad . . . but the earring was so pretty! Maybe Staci would get over it. But days went by, and Staci continued to be angry at Leanne, treating her horribly. Leanne moped around, and Lily felt worse and worse. Finally, Mom sat both girls down for a stern lecture. When she reminded them that "It's just an earring and not worth all this ugliness," Lily knew what she had to do. She got the earring out of its hiding place and pushed it through the bars of the cage. Staci heard the noise and saw the earring. "How did that get in the cage?" she asked, puzzled. Then she looked at Leanne. "No matter. I've been a brat! Can you forgive me?" "If you can forgive me. I thought I was being careful!" The girls hugged, and Mom smiled at them both. "That's much better," she said.

Once again, peace reigned. And every once in awhile, one of the girls will stop to wonder how that earring got in – and out – of the cage.

CPSIA information can be obtained
at www.ICGtesting.com
Printed in the USA
BVHW020912160919

558548BV00010B/249/P

9 781728 326719